Superhero HARRY

The Recess Bully

by Rachel Ruiz

illustrated by Steve May

PICTURE WINDOW BOOKS
a capstone imprint

Superhero Harry is published by Picture Window Books
A Capstone Imprint
1710 Roe Crest Drive
North Mankato, Minnesota 56003
www.mycapstone.com

Library of Congress Cataloging-in-Publication Data is available on
the Library of Congress website.

ISBN: 978-1-4795-9856-4 (library hardcover)
ISBN: 978-1-4795-9860-1 (paperback)

Designer: Hilary Wacholz

Printed and bound in the USA

010370F17

TABLE OF CONTENTS

ALL ABOUT
Superhero
HARRY

NAME: **Harrison Albert Cruz**

FAVORITE COLOR: **red**

FAVORITE FOOD: **spaghetti**

FAVORITE SCHOOL SUBJECT: **science**

HOBBIES: **playing video games, inventing, and reading**

IDOLS: **Albert Einstein and Superman**

BEST FRIEND, NEIGHBOR, AND SIDEKICK: **Macy**

LATEST INVENTION: **Superhero Flashlight Belt**

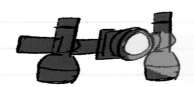

CHAPTER 1

HARRY'S SUPER HALLOWEEN COSTUME

Harry can't wait to get to school today! It's Halloween! There's going to be a party and a costume parade around school.

Harry's dressing up as Superman. His costume is almost complete. He's wearing his favorite red superhero cape from his aunt Gwen. Now he's just adding the last finishing touch.

Harry loves superheroes. He wishes he had superpowers. If he had superpowers, he probably wouldn't be so clumsy.

But since he doesn't, he builds inventions to make himself more superhero-ish.

His latest invention is his superhero flashlight belt. He made it using one of his old belts, small flashlights, and rubber bands. When he presses a button, the flashlights turn on. It helps Harry find things.

"There it is!" Harry yells, reaching for his superhero mask under his bed.

When Harry gets on the school bus, a girl dressed like Wonder Woman waves him over.

"Harry, over here!"

That's Macy. She is Harry's next-door neighbor, superhero sidekick, classmate, and best friend.

As Harry walks toward Macy, he trips on his cape. His apple rolls right out of his lunch bag and under a seat.

"Your apple!" Macy says.

"Not to worry," Harry says. "I'll find it with this."

Harry presses the button, and his superhero flashlight belt lights up. He finds the apple in a flash.

"Wow!" Macy says. "You really are like a superhero."

CHAPTER 2

THE NEW KID AT SCHOOL

At Parker Elementary everyone's wearing Halloween costumes. Melanie is a mermaid. Jackson is a cowboy.

Even Ms. Lane is wearing a costume. She is dressed like Dorothy from *The Wizard of Oz*. She's wearing ruby slippers and carrying a basket with a plush dog inside.

"Class," Ms. Lane says, "we have a new student joining us today. Please say hello to Jeremy."

"Hi, Jeremy!" the class says.

Jeremy is not wearing a costume. And he doesn't look very happy.

"Hey, Jeremy, where's your costume?" Harry asks. "Are you going to put it on after lunch?"

"What are going to be?" Macy asks.

Jeremy's response surprises Harry and Macy.

"Costumes are lame. Halloween is lame. And this school is super lame," he says, sliding down in his seat.

"Today is your first day at Parker Elementary," Macy says. "How do you know you won't like it here?"

"Just a feeling I get," Jeremy says. He looks at Harry. "What are you supposed to be anyway?"

"I'm Superman, of course!" Harry says proudly, pretending to flex his super muscles.

"His nickname is Superhero Harry," Macy explains. "And Superman is his favorite superhero."

"Superhero Harry? More like Superlame Harry!" Jeremy says as he laughs.

"Hey, that's mean," Macy says, but Jeremy turns his back to her.

Harry and Macy look at each other. Harry just shrugs.

CHAPTER 3

THE RECESS BULLY

At recess things with Jeremy don't get any better. Harry and some of his classmates are playing kickball. But not Jeremy. He's sitting under a tree alone.

"Hey, Jeremy! Why don't you join us?" Macy asks.

"Sure," Jeremy says.

"Great!" Macy says. "You can be on my team."

But instead of playing, Jeremy runs over and steals the ball. "Try playing kickball now!" he yells.

"Hey!" Ethan cries. "Bring that back!"

"What is up with that kid?" Macy asks.

"I don't know," Harry says. "But as our class superhero, I will save the day. I promise."

Harry finds Jeremy on the other side of the playground.

"That wasn't very nice, Jeremy. Can you please give me the ball back?" Harry asks.

"You'll have to find it first,"
Jeremy says.

Harry does a quick scan of the
playground. He doesn't see the
ball anywhere.

"Why don't you just use your X-ray vision to find the ball, Superman?" Jeremy asks.

That's when Harry remembers he's wearing his superhero flashlight belt! Harry presses the button, and the belt lights up.

"What is that ridiculous thing?" Jeremy asks.

"It's my superhero flashlight belt," Harry replies. "It's going to help me find the ball you took."

"Superhero flashlight belt?" Jeremy laughs. "You are super weird!"

This makes Harry even more determined to find the ball. He shines his belt toward the bushes. He immediately spots the ball.

"Found it!" Harry calls to Macy and the other kids.

"Whatever," Jeremy says as he walks away.

Harry happily brings the ball back to his friends.

CHAPTER 4

SUPERHERO HARRY WILL SAVE THE DAY

The next day at recess, things get even worse. First Jeremy steals Violet's jump rope and buries it. Then he takes Ethan's hat and hides it in a pile of leaves.

When Harry tries to get back his friends' things, Jeremy teases him. He calls him a nerd because he likes superheroes, science, and inventing stuff.

"We should tell Ms. Lane Jeremy is being a bully," Macy says.

"Not yet. Superhero Harry can still save the day," Harry says. "I just need to keep thinking."

* * *

At dinner, Harry is not hungry.

"I forgot the salad dressing," Harry's mom says.

"I'll get it!" Harry says. He runs to the kitchen, and then runs back out.

His mom says, "Please don't run or you'll drop that —"

SPLAT!

Harry cleans up the mess and sits back down.

"What's wrong?" his dad asks.

Harry tells his parents about the mean things Jeremy has been doing and saying.

"Superhero is part of my nickname, but I can't even defend myself or my friends against a bully. What kind of superhero is that?" he asks.

"Have you tried talking to Jeremy?" his mom asks.

"Kind of," Harry says. "He just ignored me. Then he was mean again."

"I think you should try again," his dad says.

"If that doesn't work, you need to tell your teacher what's going on," his mom says.

But Harry thinks his parents are wrong. He's sure only one of his superhero inventions can stop Jeremy from being a bully. He has a long night of inventing ahead of him.

CHAPTER 5

RECESS? NO THANKS.

The next day when the bell rings for recess, nobody moves.

"Time for recess," Ms. Lane says.

"No thanks, Ms. Lane," Violet says. "I think I'll stay inside and paint a picture."

"I'm going to build a fort," Ethan says. "An inside fort."

"Me too," says Melanie.

"Me three," Jackson says.

Harry and Macy know why their friends don't want to go outside for recess.

"So nobody wants to go out for recess?" Ms. Lane asks, surprised.

They hear a loud thunderclap outside, and then rain starts to pour.

"Well," Ms. Lane says. "I guess we will have an indoor recess today."

"Hooray!" everyone shouts.

Ms. Lane says she has to step out for a few minutes. When she's gone, Harry gathers everyone around. Everyone except Jeremy, that is.

"We need to do something," Harry says. "We can't let Jeremy ruin recess for us."

"But what can we do?" Violet whispers.

"Yeah, you keep saying you'll save the day," Melanie says. "What's your plan?"

"It's this," Harry says, pulling something from his backpack.

"What is that?" Jackson asks.

"It's my latest superhero invention. I made it using my old bike pump and some confetti," Harry explains.

"Does it work?" Macy asks. "I mean, have you actually tried it on someone?"

"No, but I know it will work. The next time Jeremy does something mean, I'll pump confetti at him. Confetti always puts people in a good mood," Harry says.

"You can't be a bully if you're in a good mood," Macy says.

"Harry, you might actually save the day," Ethan says.

"I sure hope so," Harry says. "After all, I *am* Superhero Harry!"

"What are you guys whispering about?" Jeremy asks.

"Nothing," Macy says.

Jeremy pulls Macy's Wonder
Woman tiara-headband off her
head. He throws it across the
room.

"Why don't you just go away and leave us alone!" Violet yells. "Nobody likes you!"

Harry is about to pump out confetti all over Jeremy. But he stops.

Jeremy is crying.

CHAPTER 6

FROM BULLY TO FRIEND

"What is going on in here?" Ms. Lane asks, walking back into the classroom.

"Everyone is bullying me," Jeremy says.

"That's not true!" Macy yells.

"He's lying!" Harry shouts.

"Calm down, class," Ms. Lane says. "Jeremy, are your classmates *really* bullying you?"

Everyone looks at Jeremy. His face starts turning red. He looks down at his feet.

"No," Jeremy quietly says. "I've been bullying them."

"It's never okay to be a bully," Ms. Lane says.

"I know. It's just something I do," Jeremy says.

"I made him cry, Ms. Lane," Violet says. "I'm really sorry, Jeremy."

"It's fine," Jeremy says.

"All right, class. Let's get back to recess and have some fun," Ms. Lane says. "Jeremy, please come see me for a minute."

Harry remembers the advice his parents gave him at dinner. He stops Jeremy.

"Jeremy, why have you been so mean to all of us?" Harry asks.

"My family moves around a lot," he explains. "It's a lot easier to leave if I don't have any friends. I learned that after my third school."

"It must be hard to always be the new kid," Macy says.

"We'd like to be friends with you, no matter how long you stay here," Harry says.

"Really?" Jeremy asks. "You want to be my friend even after I've been bullying you?"

"If you stop being a bully we would love to be your friends," Macy says.

"I'd like that," Jeremy says.

"So would I. Mission complete! Superhero Harry, over and out!"

GLOSSARY

advice — opinion about what could or should be done in a situation

bully — a person who is mean or threatening to others

clumsy — moving or doing things in an awkward way and tending to drop or break things

confetti — small pieces of colored paper thrown into the air during a celebration

defend — to make or keep safe from danger

invention — a useful new device

nickname — a name given to a person, place, or thing in place of the real name

response — written or spoken answer

scan — to look carefully or examine

sidekick — a person who helps and spends a lot of time with someone

TALK ABOUT IT

1. Should Harry and his friends have told the teacher about Jeremy being a bully sooner? Why or why not?

2. Harry and his friends tried to include Jeremy, but did they do enough? Talk about your answer.

3. Do you think Jeremy should have been punished for bullying the other kids? Why or why not?

WRITE ABOUT IT

1. Pretend you are Jeremy. Write about how you felt after your first day at Harry's school.

2. Jeremy didn't want to be a bully, but he didn't know how else to express his emotions. Make a list of ways you deal with your feelings.

3. Write a paragraph describing what would you do if you were being bullied.

ABOUT THE AUTHOR

Rachel Ruiz is the author of several children's books. She was inspired to write her first book picture book, When Penny met POTUS, after working for Barack Obama on his re-election campaign in 2012.

When Rachel isn't writing books, she writes and produces TV shows and documentaries. She lives in her hometown of Chicago with her husband and their daughter.

ABOUT THE ILLUSTRATOR

Steve May is a professional illustrator and animation director. He says he spent his childhood drawing lots of things and discovering interesting ways of injuring himself.

Steve's work has become a regular feature in the world of children's books. He still draws lots but injures himself less regularly now. He lives in glamorous north London, and his mom says he's a genius.

BE A SUPERHERO AND READ THEM ALL!

The Superhero Project
by Rachel Ruiz   Illustrated by Steve May

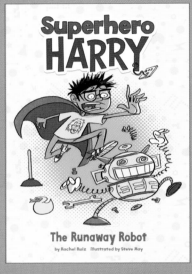

The Runaway Robot
by Rachel Ruiz   Illustrated by Steve May

The Wild Field Trip
by Rachel Ruiz   Illustrated by Steve May

The Recess Bully
by Rachel Ruiz   Illustrated by Steve May